When Cows Come Home

To Ralph and Kathleen Kennon,
for everything
             —D. L. H.

For my brother, with love
             —C. L. D.

Text copyright © 1994 by David L. Harrison
Illustrations copyright © 1994 by Chris L. Demarest
All rights reserved

Published by Caroline House
Boyds Mills Press, Inc.
A Highlights Company
815 Church Street
Honesdale, PA 18431
Printed in China

Publisher Cataloging-in-Publication Data
Harrison, David L.
When cows come home / by David L. Harrison ;
illustrated by Chris L. Demarest.—1st ed.
[32]p. : col. ill. ; cm.
Summary: A herd of cows ride bicycles, square dance, go swimming,
and more in this rhyming picture book.
ISBN 1-56397-143-7 Hardcover
ISBN 1-56397-946-2 Paperback
1. Cows—Juvenile fiction. [1. Cows—Fiction.] I. Demarest, Chris L., ill.
II. Title.
  [E]   1994 AC CIP
Library of Congress Catalog Card Number 93-70870

First edition, 1994
First Boyds Mills Press paperback edition, 2001
Book designed by Tim Gillner
The text of this book is set in 20-point Galliard.
The illustrations are done in watercolors.

When Cows Come Home

by David L. Harrison

illustrated by Chris L. Demarest

Boyds Mills Press

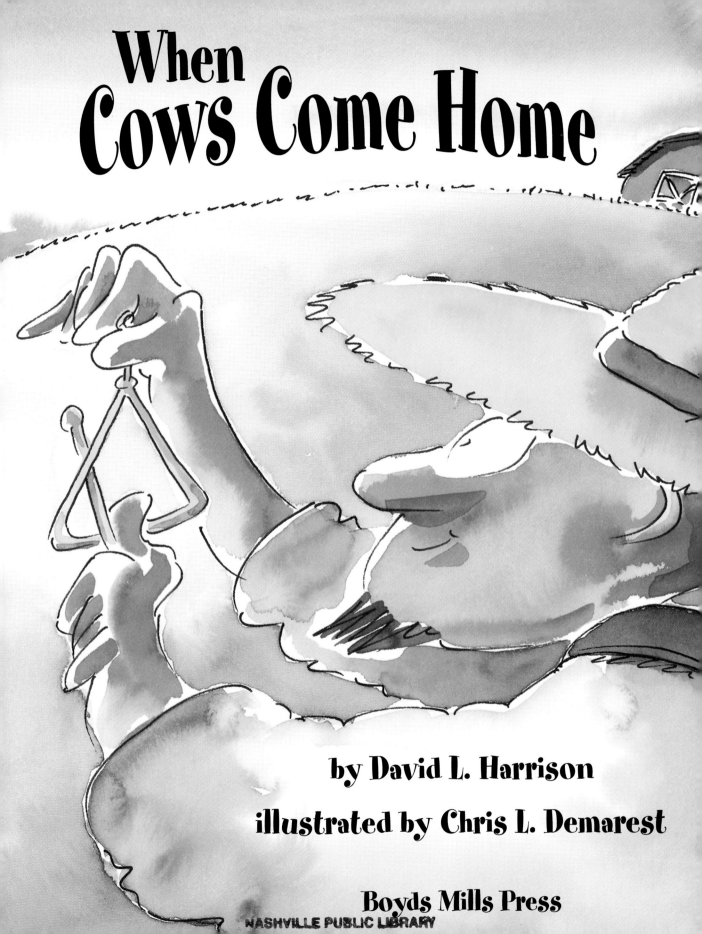

When cows come home
At the end of the day,
They swish their tails
And gently sway.

They chew their cuds
In a cowlike way,
When cows come home
At the end of the day.

But if Farmer looks
The other way,
Cows take off
On a holiday!

You never saw
Such cow horseplay,
When Farmer looks
The other way!

Cows play tag
In fields of hay.
"Catch me if
You can!" they say.

You ought to see them
Dash away,
When cows play tag
In fields of hay.

They fiddle their fiddles
And shout "Hooray!"
"Let's all sing
At the end of the day!"

"Let's square dance
With a ho! and a hey!"
And they fiddle their fiddles
And shout "Hooray!"

They hitch their bikes
To Farmer's sleigh
To pull their babies
As they play.

And who would ever
Know that they
Could ride on bikes
Or pull a sleigh!

"Everyone into the pond!"
Cows say.
"Let's cool off
At the end of the day!"

"Last one in
Is an old blue jay!
Everyone into the pond!"
Cows say.

They laugh at donkeys
When they bray
And bring them onions
For a bouquet.

They somersault
And prance away
And laugh to hear
The donkeys bray.

"Open the gate!"
"Let's run away!"
"Open the gate
So we can stray!"

"Should we leave?"
"Or should we stay?"
"Open the gate!"
"We might! We may!"

"Shhh!" they whisper
Through the hay.
"Farmer's looking
Around this way!"

"Let's swish our tails
And gently sway."
"Shhh!" they whisper
Through the hay.

Giggling softly,
Cows obey
And head for home
In a cowlike way.

Farmer winks
And milks away,
When cows come home
At the end of the day.